CARTOON NETWORK®
SCOOBY-DOO!
SNACK SNATCHER

Michelle

By Gail Herman
Illustrated by Duendes del Sur

WORLDWIDE PUBLISHING™

SCHOLASTIC INC.
New York Toronto London Auckland Sydney
Mexico City New Delhi Hong Kong

This book belong to

Michelle

No part of this work may be reproduced, stored in a retrieval system, or transmitted in any form or by any means, electronic, mechanical, photocopying, recording, or otherwise, without written permission of the publisher. For information regarding permission, write to Scholastic Inc., Attention: Permissions Department, 555 Broadway, New York, NY 10012.

ISBN 0-439-20229-9

12 11 10 9   4 5 6/0

Illustrated by Duendes del Sur
Designed by Maria Stasavage

Printed in the U.S.A.
First Scholastic printing, May 2001

![Coolsville Bake Off storefront with the Scooby-Doo gang arriving]

Shaggy, Scooby, and the gang were at the
Coolsville Bake-Off Contest.

"Like, get a noseful of that!" Shaggy sniffed
the air.

"Rmmm-rmmm!" Scooby-Doo sniffed, too.

3

Scooby and Shaggy had entered the contest.
They were going to bake Scooby Snacks.

"Like, this contest is the best!" Shaggy smiled. "The winner gets free pizza — for a year!" Fred pointed to a booth. "That's your spot," he told Shaggy and Scooby.

Velma, Fred, and Daphne grabbed the supplies.

"These bags weigh a ton!" Velma said.

"What is in here?" asked Daphne.

"Ingredients," said Shaggy ."Flour, sugar . . ."

Then Scooby pulled out a box. "Rizza!"
Scooby cried.

"There's no pizza in Scooby Snacks," Velma
said.

Shaggy took a big cheesy bite. "It's not for
the snacks," he explained. "It's for the
cooks!"

"Rat's right!" said Scooby.

"Humph!" said skinny Ms. Pinchface, in the next booth. "What noisy eating!"

Shaggy and Scooby watched Ms. Pinchface wash lima beans for a veggie pie. Then they spied the Tubb Twins, making double fudge brownies.

Shaggy reached out a hand. Scooby reached out a paw.

"Don't!" said Velma. "You can't eat anybody else's food. It's against the rules. You will be kicked out of the contest."

Daphne smiled. "But *we* can try anything we like!"

"Let's go!" Fred said.

"Like, let's get cooking!" said Shaggy. Scooby took out more ingredients. Then they pulled out baking sheets, dough cutters, chef hats, aprons, and finally: another pizza!

"Whew!" Shaggy yawned. "I'm tired. If I weren't hungry for Scooby Snacks, I would take a nap. Like, let's hurry, Scoob. So we can snooze!"

Shaggy grabbed the flour. *Splat!* It spilled on the floor. Scooby grabbed the eggs. Crack! They smashed on the table.

"Pour!" Shaggy shouted. "Knead! Mix!"

Finally, the dough was ready.
Shaggy and Scooby shoved the snacks in the
oven. In a flash, they fell asleep.

Across the room, Velma, Fred, and Daphne heard a scream and a thud. It was Ms. Pinchface, a bag of lima beans at her feet.

"What's wrong?" cried Daphne.

"There's a monster!" Ms. Pinchface shouted.

"Over by my table! It's all white and spooky-looking, without any eyes!"

A rumbling noise shook the room.

"I see something on the other side!" Daphne cried.

"Let's go!" said Fred.

Velma, Fred, and Daphne ran closer. The noise grew louder. But as they reached the cooking booth, the noise stopped. The monster was gone.

"Like, quiet down, you guys," Shaggy said. "We're sleeping here!"

"We're sorry," said Daphne.
"But Ms. Pinchface saw a
monster!" Velma added.
"A monster?" Shaggy said.
"Wake up, Scooby. There's
a monster . . . ."
Bing! The oven timer went
off.
"Ronster!" Scooby said,
and jumped up.

"That was the oven," said Velma.
Shaggy opened the oven.
"Zoinks!" cried Shaggy. "It's empty!"
"No Rooby Racks?" said Scooby.

"The monster ate your snacks!" Ms. Pinchface said.

"Like, we didn't see any monster," said Shaggy.

"Of course not," she said. "You were sleeping!"

"Look at this!" said Velma.
She pointed to handprints on the oven door — yellow ones!
"And rook!" cried Scooby. There were huge paw prints on the floor.
Monster prints!
"Let's look for clues!" said Fred.

"Scooby and Shaggy can guard the oven," Velma said.

"Not even for free pizza," Shaggy said.

"Would you do it for Scooby Snacks?" Velma asked.

Scooby sniffed hungrily. So did Shaggy.

"Rooby Racks? Rokay!"

Velma, Daphne, and Fred followed the trail of paw prints. Shaggy and Scooby were alone.

All at once, they spied a trail of crumbs.

"This could lead to the monster!" said Shaggy.

"Or more Rooby Racks!" said Scooby.

They followed the crumbs.

Scooby licked up one crumb, then another.
"Hey!" said Shaggy. "Leave some for me."
He gobbled some up, too.
Slurp, slurp. They kept their heads to the ground.

Bump! They crashed into Daphne, Fred, and Velma.

Shaggy rubbed his head. "Like, hey! We're back where we started. And so are you!"

"The crumbs circle the oven, and so do the paw prints," said Velma.

She peeked at Scooby's paws. "White!" she said. She examined Shaggy's hands. "Yellow!" she cried. Fred wiped crumbs from Shaggy's shirt.

"These crumbs are just like the ones on the floor!" he said.

"Shaggy, did you eat the Scooby Snacks?"
"Well, maybe I woke up from my nap for a minute, and ate *some*."
"What about you, Scooby-Doo?" Velma said.
Scooby shrugged. "I rate rome, roo."

"There is no monster!" Velma said. "We saw something white. But it was only Shaggy and Scooby wearing an apron and hat! Shaggy's hands are yellow from egg yolk. He made the handprints! And Scooby's paws are white from flour. He made the paw prints! You both ate the snacks. And you didn't even know it!"

"But we are out of the contest," said Shaggy.
"Now you can try all the food!" said Velma.
Shaggy took a bite of the veggie pie. "Like, this is delicious!" He eyed all the tables.
"And we've only just begun!"
Scooby grinned.
"Scooby Dooby Doo!"